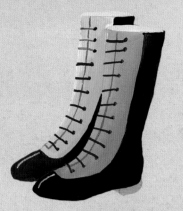

This edition published by Parragon in 2013
Parragon
Chartist House
15–17 Trim Street
Bath BA1 1HA, UK
www.parragon.com

ISBN 978-1-4723-1080-4

Printed in China

The Elves
and the
Shoemaker

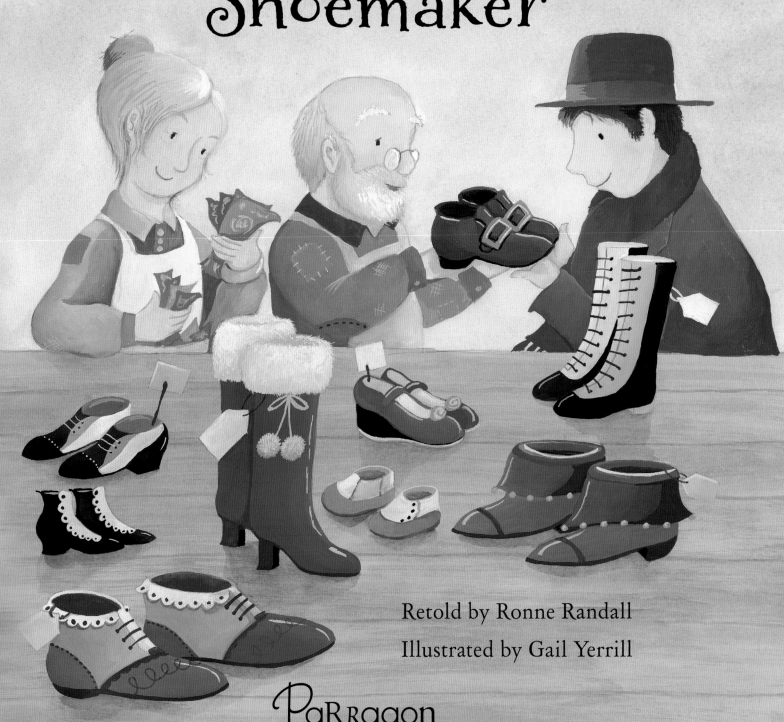

Retold by Ronne Randall

Illustrated by Gail Yerrill

PaRragon

Bath · New York · Singapore · Hong Kong · Cologne · Delhi
Melbourne · Amsterdam · Johannesburg · Shenzhen

Once upon a time, a shoemaker lived with his wife above his workshop.

The shoemaker was a good man, and he worked hard, but he was very poor. The day came when he had only enough leather to make one pair of shoes.

He cut out the leather and then left it on his workbench.

"I will be able to make a better pair of shoes after I've had a good night's sleep," he told his wife as they went upstairs.

The next morning, bright and early, the shoemaker went downstairs.

What a surprise he had!

On his workbench, where the leather had been, there was a **brand-new pair of shoes.** They were neatly and perfectly made, with not a stitch out of place.

"These shoes are masterpieces!" the shoemaker exclaimed to his wife. He put them in the window, hoping someone would come and buy them.

Sure enough, a finely dressed young man soon entered the workshop to try on the shoes. They fitted perfectly, and they were so handsome that the man happily paid a high price for them.

With the money, the shoemaker was able to buy enough leather to make two new pairs of shoes.

By the time he returned to his shop, he was tired, so he cut out the leather and left it on his workbench. Then he went upstairs to bed.

The next morning, the shoemaker had another surprise! There on the workbench were TWO new pairs of shoes! They were even more beautiful than the first pair, and were just as perfectly made.

The shoemaker put them in the window, and before lunchtime he had sold both pairs for a very good price.

Now he had enough money to buy leather for four pairs of shoes.

Once again, he cut out the leather, left it on his workbench, and went upstairs to bed.

And once again, he came down the next morning to find **beautiful shoes**, all made up and perfectly stitched.

The same thing happened every day for weeks. The shoemaker and his wife were not poor any more.

"The shoes have been appearing
as if by magic," the shoemaker said
to his wife. "But someone must have
made them. Who do you think it
could be?"

"Let's sit up tonight and watch,"
his wife suggested. "Maybe we can
find out."

So that night, the shoemaker left
some leather, all cut out and ready
to sew, on his workbench as usual.

Then, instead of going to bed, he and his
wife hid behind a curtain at the back of the shop.

There they waited ... and waited ...
and waited.

The shoemaker and his wife were just about to go to bed when, at the stroke of midnight, the shop door opened, and in danced two tiny elves! They skipped up to the workbench, and quickly began sewing the leather into fine new shoes. As they worked, they sang,

"We will sew and we will stitch,
To help the shoemaker grow rich!"

Soon the shoes were finished and the little
elves leapt off the workbench and danced out of
the shop.

"Those kind elves have helped us," said the
shoemaker, astonished. "We must repay them."

"Did you see how thin their clothes were?"
his wife asked. "And their little feet were bare!
Those poor little men must be freezing."

"Let's make some warm clothes for the elves, to
show how grateful we are," said the shoemaker.

The next day, the shoemaker's wife
knitted two cozy, woolen jackets ...

two tiny scarves ...

and two pairs of warm pants.

The shoemaker used his finest leather
to make two little pairs of boots.

That night, instead of leaving leather on his workbench, the shoemaker left the clothes, all wrapped up in shiny paper and ribbons. Then he and his wife hid behind the curtain to wait.

At the stroke of midnight, the shop door opened, and in came the little elves.

They hopped up onto the workbench, and saw the presents that had been left for them.

They opened the parcels at once, and in the twinkling of an eye, they had dressed in their brand-new clothes. They knew that the presents were the shoemaker's way of saying thank you, and they did a happy dance together, singing,

"Now the shoemaker's grown rich,
There's no need to sew and stitch."

Then they hopped off the workbench and scurried out the door.

The shoemaker and his wife never
saw the little elves again. But their
troubles were over, and they had
a good and happy life together for
many long years.

The End

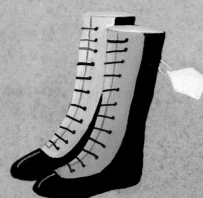